8808 Washington Wizards

8808
Joseph, Paul
Washington Wizards   J796.323 Jos

Inside the NBA
Washington Wizards

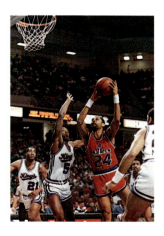

Paul Joseph

ABDO & Daughters
PUBLISHING

Published by Abdo & Daughters, 4940 Viking Dr., Suite 622, Edina, MN 55435.

Copyright ©1997 by Abdo Consulting Group, Inc., Pentagon Tower, P.O. Box 36036, Minneapolis, Minnesota 55435. International copyrights reserved in all countries. No part of this book may be reproduced in any form without written permission from the publisher. Printed in the United States.

Cover photo: Allsport
Interior photos: Allsport, pages 5, 21, 24, 27
　　　　　　　　Wide World Photos, pages 1, 8, 10, 13, 15, 23

Edited by Kal Gronvall

Library of Congress Cataloging–in–Publication Data

Joseph, Paul, 1970-
　　The Washington Wizards / by Paul Joseph
　　　　p.　cm. — (Inside the NBA)
　　Includes index.
　　Summary: Provides an overview of the history and key personalities connected with the team that has represented the nation's capital in the NBA for over twenty years and will change its name from the Bullets to the Wizards in 1997.
　　　ISBN　1-56239-778-8
　　1. Washington Bullets (Basketball team)—Juvenile literature.
2. Washington Wizards (Basketball team)—Juvenile literature.
[1. Washington Bullets (Basketball team)—History. 2. Washington Wizards (Basketball team)—History.　3. Basketball—History.]
I. Title.　II. Series.
GV885.52.W37J67　1997
796.323' 64' 09753—dc21　　　　　　　　　　96-39614
　　　　　　　　　　　　　　　　　　　　　　　　　　　CIP
　　　　　　　　　　　　　　　　　　　　　　　　　　　AC

Contents

Washington Wizards 4

From The Windy City To Baltimore 7

Continuing To Build 9

New Stars, Better Teams 11

Eastern Champions 12

From Capital To Washington Bullets 13

NBA Champions 15

The Legends Say Good-Bye 17

The No-Name Bullets 20

The Bullets Try To Build A Winner 22

Unseld Takes Over As Coach 24

Big Trade, Great Draft 26

A New Name 27

Glossary 29

Index 31

Washington Wizards

The Washington Bullets were founded in 1961 as the Chicago Packers. In their second season they were renamed the Zephyrs. In 1963, the franchise was lured to Baltimore and renamed the Bullets. Ten years later, in 1973, the Bullets moved to Washington, D.C., and to the new, larger, Capital Centre, where they were known as the Capital Bullets. They became the Washington Bullets for the 1974 season.

From 1974 to 1997, the franchise kept its name, city, and arena. But then in 1997 the team made another name change. The Washington Bullets became the Washington Wizards.

The Bullets have usually been regarded as a losing franchise, with little or nothing for fans to cheer about. But there was an 11-year period— from 1968 to 1979—when the Bullets were a winning franchise. They claimed 10 winning seasons and the 1978 NBA (National Basketball Association) Championship, with Wes Unseld and Elvin Hayes leading the way.

Facing page: The Wizards' Juwan Howard.

The next 10 years found the Bullets in the middle of the pack, finishing with 35 to 45 wins, never good enough to contend for a title, and never bad enough to a get a high draft pick.

The Bullets have tried re-building with young talent such as Kenny Green, John Williams, Muggsy Bogues, Tom Gugliotta, Calbert Chaney, Rex Chapman, and Rasheed Wallace, but nothing has worked.

The team now looks to two young stars in Chris Webber and Juwan Howard to get them back to playoff form. And that happened in the 1996-97 season. However, they ran into the Chicago Bulls in the first round and didn't stick around long. Patient fans await the return to the great decade when winning was the only way. But the return is taking a lot longer than most fans expected.

From The Windy City To Baltimore

The original Bullets franchise was born in 1961 as the Chicago Packers. The Packers not only had to vie for attention with the already established National Hockey League (NHL) Chicago Blackhawks, but also with the new upstart American Basketball League, which put a team in Chicago.

The Packers put together a decent team that was led by Walt Bellamy, the first player taken in the 1961 draft. Bellamy was second in NBA scoring with a 31-point average. Only the great Wilt Chamberlain averaged more points.

The Packers played their first game against the New York Knicks, who beat up on them 120-103. The Packers finished with only 18 wins in their first season. But considering that it was only their first year, not much more was expected from them.

They did have some bright spots—mainly Bellamy, who was voted Rookie of the Year. Besides being second in scoring, Bellamy was first in field goal percentage. He was also the West's starting center in the All-Star Game, and scored 23 points while hauling in 17 rebounds.

In the team's second season they were renamed the Chicago Zephyrs. But the bigger news was the draft pick of Terry Dischinger, who was named Rookie of the Year. With two legitimate stars in Bellamy and Dischinger, Chicago won 25 games, and looked like a franchise that was committed to building a winner.

But the commitment to winning would have to take place in another city. The Zephyrs moved their franchise to Baltimore and became the Bullets in 1963.

Walt Bellamy slams for an easy two.

Continuing To Build

The Baltimore Bullets, with their new home, continued to build and get better. In only their third season the Bullets had won 31 games.

Bellamy continued to dominate. He averaged 27 points per game and started at center in the All-Star Game over Wilt Chamberlain, who was now in the Western Conference. Dischinger also continued to improve, and he too was named to the All-Star Game.

In the 1964-65 season the Bullets won 37 games and made the playoffs for the first time. They dominated the St. Louis Hawks in the opening round, winning three games to one. Then they fell to the Los Angeles Lakers in six games in the Western Finals.

The following season the Bullets made many moves in hopes of improving the team. The biggest shock was when they sent their star, Walt Bellamy, to the Knicks for Jim Barnes, Johnny Green, Johnny Egan, and cash. The move worked, as the Bullets improved by one win for the regular season.

Jerry Sloan, Don Ohl, Kevin Loughery, and Baily Howell were the team leaders on offense. Howell and Ohl were both chosen to play in the All-Star Game. But in the playoffs the Bullets were swept by St. Louis.

In the 1966-67 season the Bullets suffered through their worst season since their founding year in Chicago, winning only 20 games.

The team was in turmoil. Bad player trades, losing players due to expansion, many coaching changes, new ownership, and even a switch to the Eastern Conference made for a horrible season.

Wes Unseld (41) leaps for a rebound in a game against the New York Knicks.

New Stars, Better Teams

In 1967-68, the Bullets regrouped and won 36 games. It wasn't good enough for the playoffs, but they were turning things around.

The biggest addition for the team was the number two pick in the draft, guard Earl "The Pearl" Monroe. He led the Bullets in scoring with a 24-point average, and was named Rookie of the Year. Monroe capped his brilliant rookie season with a franchise-record 56 points against the Los Angeles Lakers.

The following season, the Bullets again had the second pick in the draft and selected Wes Unseld. Unseld was an instant star. He won the Rookie of the Year Award and the Most Valuable Player (MVP) Award, becoming only the second player to capture both awards in one season.

With the Bullets' two stars, Monroe and Unseld, the team made a 21-win improvement for a 57-25 record. Monroe was second in scoring with a 25-point average, and Unseld was second in rebounds with 18 per game.

In the playoffs, the team had high hopes. But those hopes came crashing down as the Bullets were manhandled by the Knicks in a four-game sweep.

The following season the young Bullets had another impressive year winning 50 games. Monroe and Unseld were at the top of their game. But again in the playoffs, the Bullets were beaten by the Knicks, this time in a hard-fought seven-game battle.

Eastern Champions

The young, talented Bullets were the team to watch in 1970-71. With 42 wins they advanced to the playoffs. In the first round the Bullets won a seesaw seven-game series.

In the Eastern Conference Finals, the Bullets eliminated the defending champion New York Knicks in another seven-game struggle after falling behind, 2-0. The Bullets won with 26-, 21-, and 17-point margins before winning a tight seventh game, 93-91.

The Bullets captured their first Eastern title and were heading to the NBA Finals. After already two tough seven-game battles, the Bullets were no match for the Milwaukee Bucks, who were led by their star-center Lew Alcindor (Kareem Abdul-Jabbar). Although the Bullets were eliminated in four short games, it was still a very successful season for the team.

The Bullets made two moves the following season in a bid to win it all. The first brought Archie Clark for Kevin Loughery and Fred Carter. The second move shocked many when they traded All-Star Earl Monroe for Mike Riordan and Dave Stallworth.

The Bullets made the playoffs but were ousted in six games by the New York Knicks. After being up two games to one, the Bullets folded, losing three games in a row by large margins.

The Bullets rebounded nicely in 1972-73 to win 52 games. But again New York was their first-round playoff opponent. The Knicks had an even easier time with the Bullets, winning four games to one on their way to another NBA title.

Dave Bing looks for a teammate to pass to after saving the ball from going out of bounds.

From Capital To Washington Bullets

Owner Abe Polin moved the Bullets to Washington and to his new Capital Centre. Although the Bullets were having successful seasons, the attendance was quite low in Baltimore.

For the 1973-74 season, the team was renamed the Capital Bullets. K.C. Jones took over as head coach and the team consisted of Unseld, Elvin Hayes, Mike Riordan, Archie Clark, Len Robinson, Walt Wesley, and Nick Weatherspoon.

The Bullets' attendance rose over 10,000 per game. In their first game at the new arena more than 19,000 fans celebrated a win over the Seattle SuperSonics.

After winning 47 regular season games the Bullets again were matched against the Knicks. This time it looked good for the Bullets. But in the seventh and deciding game the Knicks came away with the victory and the series.

For the following season the Bullets were renamed one last time to the Washington Bullets. With the new name came a franchise-best 60-win season. Wes Unseld and Elvin Hayes led the way. Many believed the Bullets were the best team in basketball and could possibly win it all.

In the playoffs, it looked as though they would. In the first round they narrowly edged the Buffalo Braves in seven games, and then beat the Celtics in six games for the Eastern title. Washington was ready to finally win it all. They were the favorite going into the Finals against the Golden State Warriors. But again it wasn't meant to be. The Warriors upset the Bullets in a stunning four-game sweep.

In 1975-76, the Bullets added Dave Bing to help in the scoring department. With 48 wins, the Bullets were ready for the playoffs. In an evenly matched first-round series, Washington was edged out by the Cleveland Cavaliers in seven games.

In 1976-77, Dick Motta took over as coach, and the team added Mitch Kupchak, Larry Wright, Bob Weiss, and Leonard Gray. With Unseld, Hayes, and Bing still leading the way, the Bullets matched their 48 wins from the year before.

Washington got revenge by taking the opening series from Cleveland. In the next round the Bullets were outplayed by Houston in six games, losing the last three in a row.

NBA Champions

Before the 1977-78 season, the Bullets drafted Greg Ballard. Bob Dandridge and Charles Johnson signed as free agents. The team was hoping these additions would help them finally win a title.

Injuries and poor play gave the Bullets a mediocre 44-38 record, still good enough for the playoffs. Although there were no Bullets among the top 20 scorers, they did turn it up a notch in the post-season.

Washington began the playoffs with a sweep over the Atlanta Hawks. In the second round they manhandled the San Antonio Spurs in six games, which sent the Bullets to the Eastern Conference Finals. Against the Philadelphia 76ers, the Bullets shocked everyone by winning the series in six games and earning a trip to the NBA Finals.

Right: Greg Ballard brushes past a Chicago Bulls defender on his way to the basket.

With Unseld, Hayes, Dandridge, and Johnson leading the way, the Bullets played the Seattle SuperSonics even through six games. In the seventh and deciding game the Bullets came out on top behind the MVP performance of Unseld.

No members of the Bullets team were on the All-NBA Team, and attendance had dropped by 500 a game, but Washington still had an NBA Championship.

The following season the champs made a bid to repeat. Their 54-28 record was the NBA's best. After receiving a first-round bye in the playoffs, Washington barely got by Atlanta in a hard-fought seven-game series. They then met San Antonio, whom they knocked off in seven games.

The Bullets were on to the Finals for a rematch with the SuperSonics. The Bullets got off to a great start, winning the opener at home. The Washington fans were talking back-to-back titles, the first since the great Boston Celtics teams of the 60s. But it wasn't meant to be. The Bullets lost a shocking four games in a row and a chance at repeating.

The following year was quite a let-down for the Bullets. They made it to the playoffs behind the solid and consistent play of veterans Unseld and Hayes. But in the playoffs the Bullets were easily swept by the Philadelphia 76ers.

The Washington Bullets were now headed into the 1980s, a new decade that did not look good. The 1970s were very kind to the Bullets. They had good attendance, great players in Unseld and Hayes, super coaching, four trips to the NBA Finals, and one NBA Championship. But the 1980s would not be as kind.

The Legends Say Good-Bye

Washington began to falter. In the 1980-81 season they captured 39 wins, but missed the playoffs. Attendance really began to fall—nearly 2,000 a game.

In the 1981-82 season, the Bullets would be without their star, Wes Unseld, who retired due to injuries. The undersized, 6-foot, 7-inch but bulky center was known for his hard, consistent, and rugged play.

Unseld left the game with 10,624 points, and 13,769 rebounds. A long-time favorite of the fans and the entire Bullets organization, Unseld became a vice-president of the team in 1981. He then moved to assistant coach in 1987 and moved to head coach 27 games into the season.

Unseld was inducted into the Hall of Fame in 1988. He continues to hold close ties to the community of Washington as a volunteer for many organizations throughout the city. When people think of the Bullets, most think of the great Wes Unseld.

In the same season, the Bullets lost another great star in Elvin Hayes. Hayes was traded to the Houston Rockets for two second-round picks. After a great career Hayes was inducted into the Hall of Fame in 1990.

Mitch Kupchak was lost in the free agent market to the Lakers. With the two legends of the Bullets gone, and young Kupchak off to the West Coast, most believed the Bullets had no chance to return to the playoffs.

Washington

Walt Bellamy was voted Rookie of the Year for the Chicago Packers' 1961-62 debut season.

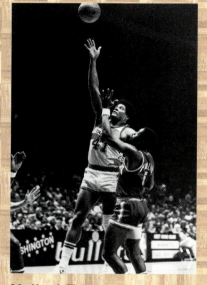

Hall-of-Famer Wes Unseld retired in 1981 with 10,624 points and 13,769 rebounds.

Jeff Malone was selected for the 1986 All-Star Game. He finished the season with a 22-point average.

Wizards

Moses Malone was an All-Star in 1986, finishing the season with a team-leading 24-points-per-game average.

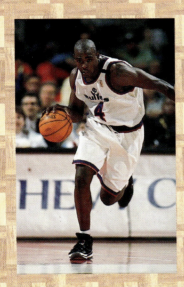

Chris Webber came to the Washington Bullets in the 1994-95 season, after winning Rookie of the Year honors playing for the Golden State Warriors.

The Washington Wizards are banking on young talent like Juwan Howard to lead them to a long-awaited championship.

The No-Name Bullets

In 1983, the Washington Bullets surprised the rest of the league by winning 43 games and making the playoffs. A group of no-names led by Frank Johnson, Charles Davis, John Lucas, Kevin Grevey, and rookie Jeff Ruland were headed to the post-season. The Bullets' surprising season, with Gene Shue awarded Coach of the Year for leading the no-names, and Bob Ferry NBA Executive of the Year for putting the team together, continued on through the playoffs.

In the first round the Bullets swept Atlanta, and were hoping to upset the heavily favored Celtics in the following round. But the Bullets were no match for the Celtics, and lost in five games.

The Bullets came back the next year with a respectable 42-40 record. Although it wasn't good enough for the post-season, many were surprised by their overall consistent play. Jeff Ruland led the team in scoring with 19 points per game.

For the 1983-84 season, the playoffs were expanded to include eight teams per conference. This gave the 35-47 Bullets, seventh in the East, a break. But future NBA Champion Boston beat the Bullets in five games. It wasn't easy for the Celtics as the Bullets played them very tough. The Bullets grabbed their one victory in overtime, and the Celtics' four wins were decided by eight points or less.

Jeff Ruland again led the way for the Bullets. He averaged 22 points per game, and 12 rebounds. Ruland was selected to the All-Star Game for his outstanding play.

The Bullets acquired Jeff Malone for the 1984-85 season. He added a much-needed lift to the offense. Malone finished the year tied with Ruland, both averaging 19 points per game.

The team finished much like the year before. They won 40 games and were matched against the heavily favored 76ers in the first round. The Sixers easily manhandled the Bullets in a four-game sweep.

Jeff Malone dribbles down the court.

The Bullets Try To Build A Winner

The Bullets were having trouble filling the seats, and winning wasn't coming easily either. For the 1985-86 season, they made many changes in hopes of building a winner. Gene Shue was given the boot and Kevin Loughery took over as head coach.

The Bullets chose Kenny Green with their first-round pick, passing on Karl Malone, who went to the Utah Jazz. Manute Bol, the 7-foot, 6-inch center, was claimed in the second round, and Dan Roundfield was acquired from the Detroit Pistons.

The changes helped very little. The Bullets wound up with 39 wins and drew the 76ers in the first round of the playoffs, and exited in five quick games.

Attendance continued to drop for the Bullets. But on the bright side, Jeff Malone was selected for the 1986 All-Star Game. Malone finished the year with a 22-point average.

The Bullets didn't give up on building. Before the 1986-87 season they acquired Philadelphia star center Moses Malone and Terry Catledge for Jeff Ruland and Cliff Robinson. First rounder Kenny Green never panned out, and he too was shipped to the 76ers for Leon Wood.

Moses Malone makes an easy slam dunk for two points.

John "Hot Rod" Williams was the Bullets' first-round pick out of Tulane University. Williams was a big-time scorer and would fit in nicely with the two Malones.

The Bullets finished the year with an impressive 42 wins on their way to the playoffs. But once again Washington was ousted in a three-game sweep by the Detroit Pistons. Nonetheless, attendance climbed more than 2,700 to record the second-best attendance figure in Bullets' history.

Both Malones had great years, each making the All-Star Team. Moses led the team with 24 points per game, while Jeff finished close behind with 22.

Pervis Ellison jumps high for a rebound.

Unseld Takes Over As Coach

All-time Bullets legend Wes Unseld was lured away from the front office to take over as head coach of the Bullets for the 1987-88 season. Kevin Loughery started the season, but after an 8-19 start Unseld became the man.

Unseld turned things around and led the team to a 30-25 record the rest of the way and got the team into the playoffs. Again the Bullets were knocked off by the Pistons in the first round. But there were some bright spots for the club.

Newcomers Bernard King and 5-foot, 3-inch Muggsy Bogues made quite an impact in the scoring and assist department. Moses Malone was again selected to the All-Star Team with a 20-point average. Jeff Malone also averaged 20 points per game.

The following year the Bullets improved two games, but this time it wasn't enough for the playoffs. After the season Moses Malone left for Atlanta and Muggsy Bogues was lost to the Charlotte Hornets in the expansion draft.

For the 1989-90 season, the Bullets drafted Harvey Grant and Ledell Eackles, who turned out to be blanks for the Bullets. Washington finished the season with only 31 wins and no chance for the playoffs.

The Bullets worked a deal for the 1990-91 season that brought number-one pick Pervis Ellison to the team. The team did not make any other big moves, and lost All-Star Jeff Malone to a trade and John Williams to an injury. The Bullets finished the season out of the playoffs with only 30 wins.

It only got worse in the 1991-92 season. The Bullets fell to 25-57 and missed the playoffs for the fourth year in a row. However, Pervis Ellison was voted the NBA's Most Improved Player. He finished eighth in blocked shots and ninth in field-goal percentage, while improving his scoring to 20 points per game, the team's best.

In the 1992 draft, the Bullets chose Tom Gugliotta with their sixth pick. The 6-foot, 9-inch forward from North Carolina State came in and made the All-Rookie Team by averaging 15 points per game.

Injuries continued to haunt the Bullets. Pervis Ellison missed 33 games because of surgery to both knees. The Bullets struggled to win 20 games.

For the 1993-1994 season the Bullets drafted University of Indiana swing-man Calbert Chaney with the sixth pick. They also traded Grant for 7-foot, 285-pound center Kevin Duckworth of the Portland Trail Blazers. The Bullets now had a solid lineup with Duckworth, Gugliotta, Chaney, and Ellison who was back from his injury. However, the team lacked consistency, and again didn't make it to the playoffs.

Big Trade, Great Draft

The Bullets were not about to give up. They made their biggest trade in franchise history in 1994-95. The Bullets gave up consistent-playing Gugliotta for the Rookie of the Year and one of the best young players in Chris Webber.

Webber was drafted by the Golden State Warriors in 1993. He had a great rookie season. However, he and head coach Don Nelson couldn't get along. Webber demanded to be traded and the Bullets were the winners.

In the draft, the Bullets chose Juwan Howard of the University of Michigan. Howard and Webber were teammates and good friends in college. The team was now looking solid and truly ready to build.

Webber led the team with a 20-point average, but again the young squad with little experience missed the playoffs.

The following year Washington looked like a solid, talented, young team. But again they sunk to the bottom and missed the playoffs. The Bullets chose Rasheed Wallace with the fourth pick. He played one year and was traded.

Chris Webber played only 15 games and was out for the season after shoulder surgery. Juwan Howard became the one-man show, but couldn't do it all himself.

A New Name

Before the 1996-97 season the Bullets thought they lost one of their stars, Juwan Howard, to the Miami Heat. Howard was a free-agent and signed a contract with the Heat, only to have it canceled by the NBA for going over the salary cap. The Bullets got a second chance and resigned their power forward.

Chris Webber came back for the 1996-97 season. He and Howard led the Bullets to a 44-38 record and a spot in the playoffs. The team also got a new floor leader in talented point guard Rod Strickland. Strickland was sent over from Portland for Wallace. The team got another boost midway through the 1996-97 season when the Bullets made a coaching change. Bernie Bickerstaff stepped down as general manager of the Denver Nuggets to become head coach of Washington.

Although Washington was ousted in the playoffs in the first round by the Chicago Bulls, the future looks very good for the team. In Webber and Howard, they have two of the best young stars in the game, and any team would love to build around them.

The Washington franchise will also try their luck with a new name. Starting in the 1997-98 season the Washington Bullets will change their name to the Washington Wizards.

Juwan Howard drives toward the hoop.

After more than 30 years as the Bullets, the front office believed that the name represented violence. The team had a contest to pick a new name. Some of the other finalists were the Dragons, Express, and Stallions. But in the end, the Wizards won out.

As the Bullets, the franchise had one great decade that was capped off with an NBA Championship. As the Wizards, with Webber and Howard leading the way, it is a sure bet that the team will soon regain that championship form.

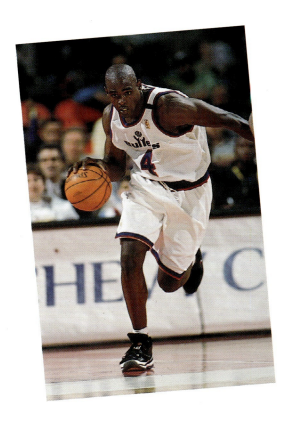

Chris Webber, along with Juwan Howard, will try to lead the newly named Wizards to an NBA championship.

Glossary

American Basketball Association (ABA)—A professional basketball league that rivaled the NBA from 1967 to 1976 until it merged with the NBA.

assist—A pass of the ball to the teammate scoring a field goal.

Basketball Association of America (BAA)—A professional basketball league that merged with the NBL to form the NBA.

center—A player who holds the middle position on the court.

championship—The final basketball game or series, to determine the best team.

draft—An event held where NBA teams choose amateur players to be on their team.

expansion team—A newly-formed team that joins an already established league.

fast break—A play that develops quickly down court after a defensive rebound.

field goal—When a player scores two or three points with one shot.

Finals—The championship series of the NBA playoffs.

forward—A player who is part of the front line of offense and defense.

franchise—A team that belongs to an organized league.

free throw—A privilege given a player to score one point by an unhindered throw for goal from within the free-throw circle and behind the free-throw line.

guard—Either of two players who initiate plays from the center of the court.

jump ball—To put the ball in play in the center restraining circle with a jump between two opponents at the beginning of the game, each extra period, or when two opposing players each have control of the ball.

Most Valuable Player (MVP) Award—An award given to the best player in the league, All-Star Game, or NBA Finals.

National Basketball Association (NBA)—A professional basketball league in the United States and Canada, consisting of the Eastern and Western conferences.

National Basketball League (NBL)—A professional basketball league that merged with the BAA to form the NBA.

National Collegiate Athletic Association (NCAA)—The ruling body which oversees all athletic competition at the college level.

personal foul—A player foul which involves contact with an opponent while the ball is alive or after the ball is in the possession of a player for a throw-in.

playoffs—Games played by the best teams after the regular season to determine a champion.

postseason—All the games after the regular season ends; the playoffs.

rebound—To grab and control the ball after a missed shot.

rookie—A first-year player.

Rookie of the Year Award—An award given to the best first-year player in the league.

Sixth Man Award—An award given yearly by the NBA to the best non-starting player.

trade—To exchange a player or players with another team.

Index

A
Alcindor, Lew (Kareem Abdul-Jabbar) 12
All-Star 7, 9, 12, 20, 22, 23, 24, 25
All-Star Game 7, 9, 20, 22, 23, 24
Atlanta Hawks 15

B
Ballard, Greg 15
Baltimore Bullets 9
Barnes, Jim 9
Bellamy, Walt 7, 8, 9
Bickerstaff, Bernie 27
Bing, Dave 14
Bogues, Muggsy 6, 24, 25
Bol, Manute 22
Boston Celtics 14, 16, 20
Buffalo Braves 14

C
Capital Bullets 4, 13
Capital Centre 4, 13
Carter, Fred 12
Catledge, Terry 22
Chamberlain, Wilt 7, 9
Chaney, Calbert 6, 25
Chapman, Rex 6
Chicago Blackhawks 7
Chicago Packers 4, 7
Chicago Zephyrs 8
Clark, Archie 12, 13
Coach of the Year Award 20

D
Dandridge, Bob 15, 16
Davis, Charles 20
Denver Nuggets 27
Detroit Pistons 22, 23, 24
Dischinger, Terry 8, 9
Duckworth, Kevin 25

E
Eackles, Ledell 25
Egan, Johnny 9
Ellison, Pervis 25
Executive of the Year Award 20

F
Ferry, Bob 20

G
Golden State Warriors 14, 26
Grant, Harvey 25
Gray, Leonard 14
Green, Johnny 9
Green, Kenny 6, 22
Grevey, Kevin 20
Gugliotta, Tom 6, 25, 26

H
Hall of Fame 17
Hayes, Elvin 4, 13, 14, 16, 17
Houston Rockets 14, 17
Howard, Juwan 6, 26, 27, 28
Howell, Baily 9

J
Johnson, Charles 15, 16, 20
Jones, K.C. 13

K
King, Bernard 24
Kupchak, Mitch 14, 17

L
Los Angeles Lakers 9, 11, 17
Loughery, Kevin 9, 12, 22, 24
Lucas, John 20

M
Malone, Jeff 21, 22, 23, 24, 25
Malone, Karl 22
Malone, Moses 22, 23, 24, 25
Miami Heat 27
Milwaukee Bucks 12
Monroe, Earl "The Pearl" 11, 12
Most Improved Player Award 25
Motta, Dick 14
Most Valuable Player (MVP) Award 11, 16

N
National Basketball Association (NBA) 4, 7, 12, 15, 16, 20, 25, 27, 28
NBA Championship 16, 28
NBA Finals 12, 15, 16
Nelson, Don 26
New York Knicks 7, 9, 11, 12, 14
National Hockey League (NHL) 7
North Carolina State 25

O
Ohl, Don 9

P
Philadelphia 76ers 15, 16, 21, 22
Polin, Abe 13
Portland Trail Blazers 25, 27

R
Riordan, Mike 12, 13
Robinson, Len 13, 22
Rookie of the Year Award 7, 8, 11, 26
Roundfield, Dan 22
Ruland, Jeff 20, 21, 22

S
San Antonio Spurs 15, 16
Seattle SuperSonics 13, 16
Shue, Gene 20, 22
Sloan, Jerry 9
St. Louis Hawks 9
Stallworth, Dave 12
Strickland, Rod 27

T
Tulane University 23

U
University of Michigan 26
Unseld, Wes 4, 11, 13, 14, 16, 17, 24
Utah Jazz 22

W
Wallace, Rasheed 6, 26, 27
Weatherspoon, Nick 13
Webber, Chris 6, 26, 27, 28
Weiss, Bob 14
Wesley, Walt 13
Williams, John 6, 23, 25
Wood, Leon 22
Wright, Larry 14